For Bella, who loves nighttime roams —H.G.

For my own wee sister, Marianna —K.G.C.

Text copyright © 2017 by Holly Grant

Jacket art and interior illustrations copyright © 2017 by K. G. Campbell

All rights reserved. Published in the United States by Schwartz & Wade Books, an imprint of Random House Children's Books,

a division of Penguin Random House LLC, New York.

Schwartz & Wade Books and the colophon are trademarks of Penguin Random House LLC.

Visit us on the Web! randomhousekids.com

Educators and librarians, for a variety of teaching tools, visit us at RHTeachersLibrarians.com

Library of Congress Cataloging-in-Publication Data is available upon request.

ISBN 978-0-553-50879-6 (hc) — ISBN 978-0-553-50880-2 (lib. bdg.) — ISBN 978-0-553-50881-9 (ebook)

The text of this book is set in 32-point Aged.

The illustrations were rendered in watercolor and colored pencil on Stonehenge paper.

Book design by Lee Wade

MANUFACTURED IN CHINA

10 9 8 7 6 5 4 3 2 1

First Edition

Wee Sister Strange

Poem by

HOLLY GRANT

Pictures by

K. G. CAMPBELL

schwartz & wade books · new york

They say there's a girl
Who lives by the woods
In a crooked old house
With no garden but gloom.

She doesn't have parents.
No one knows her name.
But the people in town
Call her Wee Sister Strange.

She climbs from her window
As the shadows grow long
And runs into the woods
Where no children dare roam.

She drinks up the moon
Like a cat drinking cream.
She drinks up the dark
Like it's tea with the queen.

She talks to the owls
In hoots and in moans.
When they've finished their dinner
She buries the bones.

Then she charms a fierce bear
While she rides on its back
Through groves golden-leafed
Under sky inky black.

When the wind starts to wuther
And the trees stir and groan
Up, up, Sister climbs
While wolves prowl down below.

She looks far and wide
Over forest and marsh.
She looks wide and far
From her high spiky perch.

She peels back the clouds:
What is it she seeks?
She peers at the stars
As through keyholes one peeks.

She dives into the bog
And she swims oh so deep
And she walks on the slime
Where the bog creatures creep.

She's searching for something.
She's searching, I'm sure!
She inspects every snail
As a mermaid counts pearls.

But her hunt leaves her stumped
Amidst bramble and thistle
Till one eve, on her wanders,
She spies the bright twinkle

Of a snug little house
With one window aglow.
Creeping up to the pane,
She peeps on tippy-toe

And there's *you* in your bed
With this book 'neath your nose!
Sister crooks her ear close
And she hears a soft voice:

"They say there's a girl
Who lives by the woods
In a crooked old house
With no garden but gloom. . . ."

She's found IT at last
In your room golden-glowing!
She's found IT at last:
A WEE BEDTIME STORY!

Her ears gobble the rhymes!
They sop up the poem-crumbs!
As the lullaby lulls,
Sister sighs and she yawns.

She snuggles beneath
Quilts of moonlight and leaves.
Her eyes shutter shut. . . .

Shhh! She's starting to dream.